Indy and Friends Save Christmas

By

Lesley Nelson

Front Cover and illustrations designed by Jan and Chris Nelson. Many thanks to them for all the beautiful illustrations.

Abundant thanks to Chris Nelson for all the technical production of my book.

Thanks to Andrea Smith for her patience and tireless work of editing.

Thanks to Katie Gardner for introducing me to Indy and for letting me use his delightful character to inspire his third story, with others to follow....

Without you all, I couldn't have brought my stories to others. You are all part of this amazing journey into publishing.

Indy and Friends Save Christmas

Indy

Hugo Mezzabron

Harry

Mabel

Toto

Blossom

Bert

Bernard

Marmaduke

Sidney

Pepito

Jim the Elf

Chapter 1

Indy, the shapeshifting hamster, and his best friends Sidney and Blossom were all sitting in front of the fire in his human parents lounge. He had lived with Katie and Martin for 18 months now.

Resting before the gas fire, the flames mesmerised them, until there was a loud knock on the door.

Martin and Katie both got up to answer the door to see who was calling at this late hour.

"My name's Mr Claus and I hear you have a rather interesting relationship with a remarkable hamster and his friends," said the large, portly, white haired old man with a fluffy white beard.

Martin stood there aghast at what the man had just said.

"What do you mean by an interesting relationship?" enquired Martin.

"I sat at the back of the cathedral praying for an answer to my problem, when a parrot landed on my shoulder, whispering in my ear, *if you are in need of help, just come outside and we can talk.*"

Mr Claus took a deep breath and pulled at his beard, then continued.

"Thinking I'd completely lost the plot, I followed the parrot outside and sat on the bench in front of the cathedral."

"Pepito," said Katie and Martin in unison.

"Yes, that's his name!" said Mr Claus.

"You better come in and sit down," said Katie.

Santa told them he'd spoken to Pepito about the problem he'd got with his Christmas deliveries and asked him if he knew anyone who could help. To which Pepito answered. "*If you've got a problem then the best thing you could do would be to speak to Indy the Hamster.*"

"Well, you can imagine at this point I thought I'd lost my mind, but I followed him to your door," Santa told them.

Katie and Martin ushered Indy over, who shapeshifted into a man, not unlike Martin in looks.

"Flipping Nora!" said Santa.

"Ah, Pepito didn't he tell you Indy is a shapeshifter then?" laughed Martin.

"No, he didn't!" answered Santa.

"Hello Santa, nice to meet you," said Indy.

Santa Claus shook Indy by the hand.

"You'll be telling me the cats talk next," muttered Santa.

"Hello, I'm Sidney and I'm Blossom," they said.

"Nice to meet you all. So how come I can understand what you are saying? I've never been able to hear a cat speak before, let alone a hamster who can change into a man."

"You must be able to talk to the Reindeer and the Elves," said Indy.

"Yes, but I've never been able to understand any other animals."

"The fact is, at this moment, you need to. Therefore, you can. It's like Katie and Martin gained the ability to understand us, but not all animals. They'd go bonkers otherwise," said Indy.

"So, how can we help you?" asked Martin. "Or should I say how can Indy help you?"

"The thing is, I've got a problem, well, quite a few actually. Rudolf the red nose reindeer has got a nasty virus and can't lead the others. In addition, I usually get some of the elves from my workshop to sort the Christmas presents ready for each house while out on the sleigh. Unfortunately, they've gone on strike for more pay.

9

Apparently danger money should be paid to anyone who flies on a sleigh. I keep telling them that money is short. Its tough just getting all the presents and paying wages as it is, but do they listen? No!" explained Santa.

"So you need our help delivering the presents?" asked Indy.

"Yes, if you can magic up a red nose reindeer with a brain like a satellite navigation system and a few elves to help me deliver the presents on time," said Santa.

"I may have a solution," announced Indy.

"I do hope so, I've got a reputation to keep."

"What's the plan Indy?" said Blossom. "Can I help?"

"Me too! I want to help," added Sidney.

"We must bring Santa to the wood. I need to discuss a plan I'm thinking of with my friend and mentor Mabel," said Indy.

Leaving Katie and Martin behind, the others went through the wood at the back of the house. Lots of animals watched them go by and Toto the rabbit seeing his friends, followed on behind. On reaching Mabel's tree house, the group soon realised they'd been followed by lots of other animals including squirrels, rabbits, sleepy hedgehogs, hares, a ferret family and several birds, including Bernard the rook.

"I'm at your service, Indy," Bernard told him.

Mabel came to the door, totally surprised by the gathering in front of her house.

"What the heck is that?" shouted Santa, before he regained his manners and composure.

"Hello, Santa Claus, I am Mabel, the renowned Wizard Owl."

She stood there, a rather tall owl wearing a cloak which appeared to show a swirling galaxy beneath.

"You don't remember me, do you?" she added.

"I certainly don't. I would've remembered you, if I'd met you before," muttered Santa.

"Cast your mind back a few years when you were searching for a new sleigh." said Mabel.

"Ok," Santa Claus replied.

"I took you around the workshop and sold you the one you use now," said Mabel, smirking.

"My memory is very good and I distinctly remember being served by an ordinary old lady whom I've known for years." replied Santa.

"Did she look like this?" asked Mabel as she shapeshifted into the old woman.

"I wish you lot would stop doing that, it's giving me heart palpitations," he snapped. "It's Christmas Eve in a few days and there are a world of children's presents to deliver."

"Sorry, please accept our apologies," Indy told him.

Mabel and Indy agreed on a plan of action. Indy would lead the reindeer by shapeshifting into Rudolf and Bernard the rook would assist with directions.

"I also need some help with getting the presents ready," added Santa Claus.

"Ah yes, as you can see there are lots of animals, who I'm sure are willing to help." Indy nodding towards the gathered throng.

"I see," said Santa. "That's nice of them to offer, but they haven't got proper hands!"

"You are rather grumpy, Mr Claus," grumbled Toto. "I will tell you now, we've all become very adept at using our paws and claws, in new and sophisticated ways."

Mabel had to stifle a laugh at the posh way Toto put over his annoyance.

"I'm so sorry, my friend. I didn't mean to be rude. It's just I am completely stressed out to the point bits of my beard are falling out and I can't be a beardless Santa, can I?" he cried.

Everyone huddled close to Santa as Toto shouted, "group hug everyone."

"Thank you, all of you. I know I'm in good hands, paws, claws, feet and, everything," mumbled Santa, sniffing loudly to hold back his tears of gratitude.

"Right Santa, where is your sleigh and how do we get to it?" asked Indy.

"Ah, there's the thing, I got it as far as the South Pole, so I'd be ready to start in the earliest time zone for Christmas Eve," he replied. "Then the strangest thing happened. I came upon this, well, it was like a man with a bear bottom."

"A bare bottom," laughed Sidney, "what a sight."

"Not a bare bottom, silly, his bottom half being a bear. He introduced himself as Hugo Mezzabron and said he couldn't help me himself, but he knew someone who could. Well, you can imagine by then I thought I'd completely lost the plot." Santa wiped his brow and continued to speak, "I'm feeling a bit hot just telling you about it."

Mabel brought him a glass of water from her kitchen. Santa thanked her and continued.

"He told me he had a shuttle craft and would be able to drop me off at the outskirts of a town, where I had to make my way to a cathedral. On arrival I'd be contacted and led to someone who could help me. It all sounded a bit bonkers."

"Did he know what your problem entailed?" asked Mabel.

"He did, but seemed a little distracted and began talking to a cat. At which point I decided to close my eyes and try to sleep," muttered Santa. "Anyway, he landed his craft in a deserted car park, let me off and left me there! Thankfully, I could see an immense structure with a spire in the distance and headed for it hoping it was the cathedral he had mentioned. The rest brought me here."

Chapter 2

Mabel called Indy over to one side.

"I know what you're going to say," said Indy. "Why was Hugo so distracted? In any case, if we're going to get Santa back to the South Pole by Christmas Eve, we'll need Hugo's craft to get us there."

"Just give us a minute Santa, we've got to make some enquiries. Toto, fetch Santa some of my apple biscuits, you'll find them in the store cupboard," said Mabel.

Indy followed Mabel into her living room and saw her go over to a large glass triangle. She picked up a wooden stick and chimed the three sides twice. Waiting a moment, then doing the same thing again. The middle of the triangle shimmered and Hugo's face appeared.

"Good evening Mabel," he said. "Is there a problem?"

"You sent Santa to Indy, were you too busy to help?" asked Mabel.

"The thing is, I had a meeting with the Wizarding Council about your use of magic outside the wood. The council weren't too happy, so I went to gloss things over," replied Hugo.

"I've never heard of a meeting in the South Pole before?" said Mabel.

"The meeting wasn't in the South Pole. I'd just gone there to meet a friend, when I was called to the meeting. But then I met Santa and needed to help him get to you."

"We need to get back to the South Pole now so we can assist Santa with his Christmas deliveries. Can you pick us up in this craft he mentioned?" Indy asked.

"I can be there at dawn and will land near my house. Could you meet me there?" asked Hugo.

"We can," replied Indy.

A flash and his image disappeared.

"What an amazing piece of technology," Indy said.

"Wow, it's incredible!" exclaimed Bernard.

"Bernard, you are the nosiest bird I've ever met. Haven't you heard of privacy," grumbled Mabel.

"I can't help myself, sorry!" sniffed Bernard.

"Ok, but be careful what you're listening in too. One day you may hear something you wished you hadn't," answered Mabel.

As Indy, Mabel, and Bernard walked out of the tree house, Santa looked up with a hopeful expression on his face, while flicking pieces of biscuit from his beard.

"So, what happens now? Can you get me back to the sleigh and help me out? When can we get going? There's not much time and I need to prepare and…"

Indy interrupted his panicked flow.

"Santa, calm down, you're getting yourself in a state. We've got a lift arranged to get back to the sleigh and I myself will select the team to go with us. Hugo will arrive at dawn. In the meantime, Mabel will take you to her guest room to lie down."

"I won't even fit inside the trunk of the tree, never mind lie down," said Santa, patting his portly tummy and chest and letting out an enormous laugh.

Sidney and Blossom were nearly blown over by the gust of breath from Santa's laugh.

"He's a bit overwhelming isn't he," said Blossom, "certainly a larger than life kind of man."

"Yeah, but what an incredible man. Working all year round to make sure children can receive their presents on Christmas morning," remarked Sidney. "I'm in awe of him."

"I do hope we get to help. What an adventure!" gushed Blossom.

"It certainly would be, my darling Blossom," replied Sidney. Sidney was so in love with Blossom, her long grey and cream fur shone and her amazingly fluffy tail hypnotised him. A handsome cat himself, they made a perfect couple. Yet Sidney's personality, kindness and how he made her laugh were the things Blossom admired.

Mabel assured Santa he would indeed fit into her home and her guest room. After a draft of her herbal tea he soon fell asleep, snoring loudly.

Indy and Sidney decided to go back to update Katie and Martin, whilst Blossom returned to the cathedral to show her face at her human home.

Early the next morning, on her way back to Katie's house to pick up the others, she became aware of Marmaduke by her side.

"Are you sure Mabel will be able to do the time changer thingy?" asked Marmaduke. "I'm very important to the Cathedral, I'll be missed," added Marmaduke, as his tail made a flourishing wave in the air.

"I do hope so!" exclaimed a voice behind them.

Bert stood there all dressed up in his cathedral suit and tie, smiling from ear to ear.

"Oh Bert, I'm so glad you came," said Blossom sweetly. "How did you know to come?"

"It was Bernard, he can't help himself. If he's heard something exciting, he has to tell others," replied Bert.

17

As if by coincidence Bernard landed on Bert's shoulder.

"Are we alright? I can't wait to help Santa deliver his presents. I'll see you back at Mabel's," Bernard said, as he flew off.

After a short chat with Katie and Martin, Indy, Sidney, Blossom, Marmaduke and Bert made their way to Mabel's.

There was lots of excitement in the wood as the animals waited for dawn to arrive. They all wanted a chance to see Hugo's shuttle craft.

When everyone had returned, Indy shapeshifted into a man to assist in talking face to face with Santa. He announced his team consisted of Bert, Toto, Bernard, Sidney, Blossom and Marmaduke. He went over his plan, telling them he was going to shapeshift into a reindeer and assume Rudolf's place. Bernard would be attached to his reins and would assist with navigation. Bert would pass the presents for each house to Santa to deliver and Sidney, Blossom, Marmaduke and Toto were to be busy getting them into address order for each drop off.

Leaving behind Mabel and the other animals, Santa and his crew went through the wood to Hugo's house waiting for his craft to arrive. Out of nowhere, a craft appeared. It looked shiny and new and resembled a small space shuttle. The door opened and a ramp came down with Hugo coming out to greet them.

"He really has got a bear bottom," Sidney laughed.

"Shush," said Indy.

"Hello again, Santa." Hugo held out his hand in greeting. "I see you've got the help you needed."

"Yes thank you. Would we be able to leave straight away?" asked Santa. "I must get to the South Pole to pick up the sleigh to begin my deliveries. Time is of the essence. From there the first stop is the Republic of Kiribati in the Pacific."

The group followed Santa and Hugo onto the craft and were shown to their places. All gasped at the size of the crafts interior, as it was far bigger than they'd imagined. Everyone made ready for takeoff, just as a large black cat appeared on the screen in front of them.

"Hello, my name is Harry, please engage the seat belts, armrests down and relax. In case of emergency, I will be here to assist you. We will take off in 10 seconds, 10, 9, 8, 7, 6, 5, 4, 3, 2, 1, take off!"

Chapter 3

The surge in speed took them all by surprise, except for Santa who had already been on the shuttle craft previously.

"Ooh gosh, that made my tummy go funny," said Toto.

"Mine too," added Marmaduke.

"Wow, I love it," beamed Bert. "It's so exciting."

Harry, the cat, came out from behind the console.

"Hello, are we all ok out here? Would you like a drink?"

"How lovely," expressed Blossom. "I think Sidney would like some too."

Lifting his head, Sidney asked. "Is there anything to eat? I feel a bit peckish."

"Hugo will sort you out. I must return to the console to monitor our progress towards the South Pole."

Hugo came out of one of the other rooms with all manner of food to suit each animal and a big bowl of stew for himself and Bert.

Santa then entertained them with a funny story about getting stuck down a chimney.

"It happened like this," said Santa. "I was doing well with my deliveries, all the chimneys were exactly the same and I fitted in them perfectly. Until I got to a large house in Bunglestone, rural England. It seemed a little different, it had new windows, which looked rather pretty. There were twinkling lights and you could see the Christmas tree inside."

"Then what happened," asked Blossom, eagerly wanting to hear the funny bit, she assumed was coming.

"I went round the back of the house to climb up the ivy trellis but guess what?"

"No ivy trellis?" asked Marmaduke.

"Oh yes, the ivy trellis was there, but the chimney I usually used was not!" exclaimed Santa.

"What did you do?" asked Indy.

"I was flummoxed at first, but what could I do? I climbed up the trellis to see if the other chimneys were still there and they were."

"Thank goodness!" Sidney chimed in.

By now all eyes were on Santa.

"But there was a problem, the chimneys left were rather narrower than my not so willowy frame," laughed Santa.

"Oh gosh, what did you do?" asked Hugo.

"Well, I had to go down one of them, so I slid down the first one and started to descend. I came out into a large fireplace and the elves lowered the presents down in a basket. I made my way over to the most beautiful Christmas tree I've ever seen. I left the presents underneath and quietly went back to ascend the chimney," said Santa.

Santa cleared his throat nervously and continued.

"Now, the descent went quite well, but going back up, not so much. I kept slipping, I just couldn't get a foot hold. I started to panic as you can imagine. Finally though, I began to move and was about halfway, when disaster struck. I was wedged in place, I couldn't go up or down."

There was an audible gasp around the shuttle craft.

"I shouted up to my elves and they just laughed at me, which didn't help. Then they had an idea. They'd go down the other chimney and try to push me up from below. It's a wonder that we didn't wake up the house with their giggling. Still, I was stuck fast, and I began to panic."

"Oh my giddy aunt," exclaimed Indy. "How did you get out?"

"Don't laugh," said Santa, "but the elves came down the chimney and tied ropes to my sturdy belt. Untethered the reindeers from the sleigh, attached the rope to them and I was pulled out like a cork from a champagne bottle."

The whole room filled with laughter and Santa smiled from ear to ear.

"Its alright for you lot, the elves have never let me forget it."

"Nevertheless, I love my job" said Santa. "I just wish I could hang about to see the children's faces on Christmas morning opening their presents. They are the reason I keep doing my job, year after year. Children are the future generation. The world depends on them to enjoy the best childhood, so that they grow up to be good and responsible adults."

"If we behave, can we come with you on a delivery?" asked Sidney.

"Let me think about it!" laughed Santa.

Toto had fallen asleep on Bert's knee and Bert stroked his back gently.

"I think he got over excited by being allowed to come," said Indy. "I had to stop him running round Mabel's tree, as he'd already made a groove in the undergrowth."

Harry called Indy and Hugo over to the console.

"Everything ok Harry?" asked Indy.

"Yes and no," answered Harry. "Yes, we're on the approach to the South Pole, but no, we've been detected on radar. I hear they're sending helicopters to check on us."

"We can't be seen!" exclaimed Hugo. "I don't understand it, we've never been spotted before.

All of a sudden, the whole craft shuddered and the internal lights flickered off and on.

"Sorry!" shouted Harry. "Just trying to kick-start the cloaking device. We need to become invisible to radar again. Phew, I'm glad to say it's worked."

"What the heck just happened?" yelled Santa.

Toto now awake, sat up hitting his head on Bert's chin, nearly knocking him out.

"It's ok," consoled Indy. "Just a technical issue. We are about to land near Santa's sleigh, so get ready to disembark."

An audible sigh reverberated around the craft.

The shuttle touched down on a patch of hard snow, coming to a halt with a slight skid.

"Sorry folks, a bit slippery this snow stuff," purred Harry.

Hugo and Harry took them to the exit door and lowered the ramp to see them safely onto the snow covered landscape. They all waved goodbye and thanked Hugo and Harry for the lift.

The group huddled round Santa and Indy, then out of nowhere there appeared a cave entrance.

"Follow me," said Santa. "The sleigh and the other reindeer are through here."

Strangely, no one felt the cold even though it was -25 degrees.

"I thought my paws would stick to this ice," said Sidney.

"Ah, it's because of my presence Sidney and friends," explained Santa. "All creatures when with me are protected from the climate and its elements.

"How amazing Santa," remarked Indy. "The universe surprises me every day with the abilities it bestows on us."

The group followed Santa into the cave and there was an audible gasp. Before them stood eight magnificent reindeer, all adorned with their Christmas finery.

"Let them introduce themselves," Santa whispered.

One after another each reindeer said their name and bowed their heads. Dasher, Dancer, Prancer, Vixen, Comet, Cupid, Donner, Blitzen.

"Most honoured to meet you all," said Indy.

"Indy here is going to take Rudolph's position," advised Santa.

"But he's a human!" grumbled Dasher.

Indy shapeshifted into a large reindeer, which made the other reindeer step back.

"Very impressive," commented Dancer.

"Yeah, but is he any good at flying?" asked Prancer.

"Yeah, can you do that?" teased Blitzen.

"He can do anything he wants. He has amazing powers and he's here to help, so stop complaining." snapped Sidney.

"It's ok Sidney, the reindeer are just a bit stressed out at the moment, as the elves have been giving them a hard time for not joining the strike," said Santa.

Santa showed the group the sleigh, which had been hidden out of sight behind the reindeer.

"Oh my goodness!" exclaimed Blossom. "It's ginormous."

Marmaduke overwhelmed, walked around it one way, then the other.

"Where do we sit?" asked Bert.

"Just let me get Indy tethered together with the others," advised Santa. "Then Bernard, you hop onto here at the side of Indy and we'll get you safely secured."

Sidney and Blossom stood close together with Bert, Marmaduke and Toto.

"I'm starting to wonder if I should've stayed at the cathedral?" said Marmaduke. "I'm not very brave. I make out I'm full of confidence, but it's only because I know my surroundings there and people love seeing me."

Bert smiled at Marmaduke and stroked his furry ginger head.

"You'll be fine my friend. I'll look after you and think of all the tales you'll be able to tell the animals at the cathedral." whispered Bert.

"Thanks Bert, I've always appreciated your kindness to me. I'm now famous because of you pointing out to visitors, how I patrol the cathedral with attention and care," said Marmaduke.

"Right guys," urged Santa. "We must leave in the next 10 minutes or we will be behind with deliveries and as you know, the children must never see me, as it all adds to the magic of Christmas."

Santa checked the tethers and secured all the reindeer, including the shapeshifted Indy, who looked most noble with all his Christmas finery. Bernard, now secure, was wearing a small red hat and miniature bells around his ankles.

"Are you alright with the directions Bernard?" asked Indy.

"Yes thanks, with my internal navigation prowess and the magical download you and Santa did together, I've got the whole earth covered."

Santa sat in the front with Bert beside him, Bert resplendent in his red suit and glitter in his hair. Blossom, Sidney, Marmaduke and Toto had red collars covered with sparkly jewels and tiny bells. As directed they jumped up onto the seats behind Santa and Bert, then all secured their safety belts.

"Now, is everyone aboard and presents secured?" asked Santa.

"All secured Santa," said Donna

"Your side Cupid?"

"Yes Santa," answered Cupid.

"Oh a Cupid," said Sidney, looking deep into Blossom's eyes.

"I think you've gone past the cupid point," said Toto. "I've never seen two cats more in love than you two!"

"Aww thank you," murmured Blossom.

"Enough of the gooey stuff, we've got work to do!" asserted Santa.

Vixen turned her head towards the cats and whispered, "don't worry he's not mad at you lot, he just takes his job very seriously and wants us to be perfectly on time."

"Right Indy, Bernard, Dasher, Dancer, Prancer, Vixen, Comet, Cupid, Donner and Blitzen are we ready for flight?" asked Santa.

"We are," they said in unison.

"First stop is Kiritimati, a small island in the Pacific Ocean," said Santa. "Take flight!"

Chapter 4

With a shudder, the sleigh rolled forward to the cave entrance, then took to the skies with Indy leading and Bernard giving him directions.

"Wow, this is incredible," Indy told Bernard between breaths. "I'm so glad we could help Santa, it's such an honour."

The cats and Toto the rabbit got the first deliveries ready for Bert to hand to Santa. The sleigh landed and Santa took the presents and made his first deliveries. Up and down the sleigh went arriving at every house, till the back of the sleigh looked a little empty.

"Oh my goodness," announced Toto, "we're only on the first island and we've nearly run out of presents."

"Oh don't worry," said Bert, "Santa told me that when the presents were getting low, I'm just to push this button and it will upload the next lot into the sleigh. Magic at its purest."

"Wow," purred Marmaduke, "this is so amazing. Look at this beautiful island and think of all the children fast asleep waiting for Santa to visit."

Santa returned to his sleigh and advised Indy that there was one more stop to make at a children's hospital.

Tears welled up in Indy's eyes as he thought of the children at the hospital. Young children all poorly and hoping to get better. He wished he could make them all well with his magic powers, but he did not have healing powers. Regaining his composure, he led the other reindeers to the last drop off point.

As Santa took the final presents into the hospital, Bert pushed the button to upload the next batch of presents. Sidney, Blossom, Marmaduke and Toto had got into a good routine of getting the presents into the order Santa wanted. So as soon as Santa got back, it was off to New Zealand.

As the sleigh flew over the ocean, everyone could see the lights of the ships on the sea and the planes in the sky.

Bernard began telling Indy how exciting it was being a bird.

"It gets me every time on a long flight, seeing the beauty of the earth from above. Having the air beneath your wings, it's awesome," said Bernard.

Santa told them about NORAD, The North American Aerospace Defense Command which tracked his journey every year.

"This means children can see where I am at any given time on Christmas Eve. Yet, NORAD is not able to give an exact time I'll arrive at a certain area, as only I know that," Santa said beaming from ear to ear.

Deliveries started on the North Island of New Zealand, then the South Island. They kept a fast pace and were soon flying over the ocean to the next stop, which was Australia.

A vast continent of its own, it was going to take a while to cover, but Santa was raring to go again. No one knew Santa's age, but he certainly had a lot of energy!

"Flipping heck, I don't know how he does it," commented Bert. "I'm just worn out handing over the presents."

"Me too," added Toto. "Every time we think we've got to the bottom of this batch of presents, loads more are uploaded."

"You need to rest one person every 10 minutes. A power nap works well I find." answered Bert. "Australia is huge, so there will be lots of uploads."

All over Australia they went with Santa keeping up the pace. Finally, he left the last house and they rose up again into the sky towards the next country.

Everything was going as planned, when suddenly an elf jumped up from within the presents.

"Why are you doing this? You should be on our side. Refuse to do this without danger money," the elf said.

"You little scoundrel, what are you doing here, I'm not having you ruin Christmas. The children are waiting for their presents and I'm not going to let a naughty elf stop me." shouted Santa.

"Yeah buzz off," yelled Toto, "you little pip squeak."

"Who are calling a little pip squeak, take it back or I'll eject you from the sleigh." cried the elf.

"I will not!" retorted Toto.

What a kerfuffle, Toto suddenly appeared up in the air. The elf tried to grab his feet, but Toto fell overboard.
Bert tried to catch Toto but failed. Without asking Santa, Indy flew down and tried to get underneath Toto to catch him with the sleigh. The other reindeers obviously followed. The whole sleigh rocking through the air.

NORAD noticed Santa's sleigh appeared to be out of control. So dispatched the nearest F16 to go and investigate.

In the meantime, mayhem began on the sleigh. Marmaduke and Sidney had the elf pinned to the floor of the sleigh, with Blossom tying him up in a length of sparkly rope from the side of the sleigh.

"Get off me you fleas ridden cats. I'll have you know I'm a major elf," he hollered

"Not anymore Jim!" said Santa. "I will be demoting you when we get back."

"You can't do that!" shouted Jim.

"I can and I will," replied Santa.

Indy tried hard to get directly underneath the falling Toto. He was just above the sleigh when Indy gave the order to stop. The other reindeers nearly ended up with their noses being stuck in one another's tails.

Bert saw Toto coming down straight above him and caught him in a blanket he'd had on his knee. Toto felt so relieved he lay in Bert's blanket for a good half hour afterwards.

"I thought I was going to... I can't say the word," cried Toto, with his eyes watering up. "Thanks for catching me. I know it wasn't an easy thing to do."

"We've caught the culprit and tied him up," said Marmaduke.

"Thank you all so much," sniffed Toto.

"What the heck is that!" shouted Sidney, as an F16 flew past.

Oh, it's just NORAD checking I'm ok," answered Santa, waving at the pilot, shooting passed on the other side. "Probably wondered why the heck I'd been zigzagging across the sky on their radar!"

After this little drama, Santa eventually calmed things down. Indy and Bernard were great together and had got the right addresses most times. Sometimes though they had to double back, much to everyone's amusement.

Santa was happy with their progress and had covered a lot of places, when another disaster struck. Comet began coughing uncontrollably just before it was time to set off to Japan.

Chapter 5

Santa got off the sleigh and ran to him.

"Comet, what's wrong?" asked Santa.

"I can't seem to get my breath and I feel so exhausted," coughed Comet.

Indy turned round and looked straight at Bert.

"Bert, can you take over from Comet," said Indy.

"A man can't take over from a reindeer, Indy. Have you lost your mind?" said Santa.

Bert stepped down from the sleigh and immediately shapeshifted into another reindeer.

Santa nearly fell over saying. "I really wish you lot would warn me when

you're going to do that, it scares the heck out of me."

"Ok I'll untether Comet and get you tethered up Bert. I'll be one man down though," added Santa.

"If you'll untie me, I'll help," urged Jim, the elf.

"Not on your Nelly, Major Jim. I'm sorry, but for now you've lost my trust," replied Santa.

Jim looked sad and tears rolled down his face, as Blossom went to sit next to him.

"He hates me now, I'll never be trusted again. I'm a good elf really, I got consumed by the thought of earning more money and I really thought we deserved it. I just went about it the wrong way," sobbed Jim.

Santa relented and untied him, Jim then took Bert's place on the front seat.

"You better behave, I still haven't forgiven you my lad. You must promise to never do such a thing again. You will be mucking out the reindeers for a few weeks, as a result! Yes and apologise to Toto too."

"Sorry Toto. I didn't really mean for you to go over board. Believe me mucking out the reindeer's is a real penance!"

Toto laughed and said, "It's ok Jim, thankfully I lived, so all is forgiven. I'll certainly never forget you though."

"We still need to recover Comet to the North Pole," said Indy.

"We haven't got time to take him," replied Santa.

"I may know of a solution," Indy told him.

"Oh I do hope so, as I don't really want to leave Comet here till Christmas Day, especially on his own. He's not well enough, but we need to deliver these presents, I don't want to disappoint the children." and he sobbed into his beard.

Indy explained to everyone about their individual signatures.

"The thing is," explained Indy. "Each of us has a unique cosmic signature. Inside every living being there is a cosmic signature, which can harness its connection to the universe."

"What are you talking about Indy? Cosmic signatures really! I've been around a heck of a long time," said Santa, "and I've never heard of such a thing, we are wasting time!"

"I beg to differ, I'm trying to help Comet, so you won't be delayed."

"Yeah, let him speak Santa, this is important to us," added Blitzen. "I'm not moving till we've found a way of getting Comet home, so the vet elf can help him."

All the other reindeer agreed.

"Please stay as still as you can and close your mind to everything but my voice and concentrate," announced Indy. "Think back to your first memory, concentrate further, go further inside, be aware of the innermost part of your being. There is a light, it's very faint, can you see it? Now, reach in and pick up the light, ok put it down again and slowly come back out and when you are out, say yes."

A resounding "Yes" echoed out.

"I'm going to try to contact Harry on the shuttle craft to come to pick up Comet. They will fly him back to the North Pole vet hospital," advised Indy. "I've never used this way to contact anyone before, but I believe I can do it. I will focus your signatures into space and attach my message."

"We're ready Indy," said Santa, nodding at the others.

"Ok, stand very still and reach into your innermost being and pick up the light you found earlier and when I say now, pick it up and throw it to me with your mind. Now!" shouted Indy.

A blast of visible light hit Indy and made him glow like the sun. He stood perfectly still and a voice spoke as if from the sky itself.

"This is Harry, can I be of assistance?"

Then there was silence. Indy glowed again.

"Yes Indy, your coordinates are locked in. I will be there shortly."

Indy fell to the ground breathing hard, still as a reindeer, his breath visible and his head wet with sweat. Santa gently stroked his head and helped him to stand up.
Blossom pointed up to the sky as a shuttle came into view.

"Look it's Harry, he's here already. Well done Indy, you did it, you really did it," said Blossom.

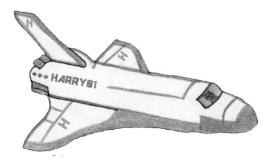

The shuttle landed and Harry came down the ramp with Hugo running after him.

"Indy, where are you?" asked Hugo.

"Here, I'm a reindeer," explained Indy.

"Me too," said Bert.

"I hear there is a poorly reindeer who needs to get to the vet hospital as soon as possible?" said Hugo.

Hugo walked over to Comet who was breathing and then coughing in equal measure.

"Come along with us Comet, we'll have you at the hospital in no time," promised Hugo.

"Thanks," said Indy. "I really appreciate your help."

"Never heard of the cosmic signatures being used in such a way before. Clever thinking Indy," nodded Hugo.

The shuttle lifted off and disappeared out of sight.

Chapter 6

"Right, there's no time to lose," announced Santa. "Japan next stop. Indy, Bernard, let's go."

The sleigh flew high into the sky, the crew all enjoying the ride.

"Isn't this just amazing!" said Toto. "From this night forward, I will think of Santa, his reindeers and his elves doing this trip year after year and know we were once part of it."

"We're so lucky," agreed Marmaduke. "Plus, we're only part of the way round yet."

"It's amazing," smiled Blossom, "look over there at all those ancient Japanese buildings, look Sidney, oh I'm so glad we came along."

Sidney moved up closer to Blossom and said. "I'm so glad we were able to witness this together."

"Oh you two love birds, you are so soppy, but I love it," murmured Toto.
"Really it's embarrassing," chirped in Jim.

"Aww leave them alone," said Santa. "It's very romantic up here with the stars twinkling."

"Coming to our next stop, Santa," said Indy. "We will get as close as possible."

"Then it's the first two doors on the right Santa," added Bernard.

The cats and Toto passed the presents to Jim, who then gave them to Santa as requested. All over Japan they flew, working hard to keep to schedule.

As the sleigh rose further up into the sky, Indy shouted he'd noticed some bad weather up ahead.

"I think it's about to blow my feathers off. Are you sure I'm secured enough Santa?" asked Bernard.

Then it came, a harsh wind with snow and hail.

"I can't see properly," shouted Bernard. "Indy, can you see anything?"

"I am fighting this oncoming wind. What do we do Santa?" he asked.

"Slow down, we need to get below this storm. Descend Indy, I'll tell you when to level off," replied Santa.

Prancer said "This weather is really unusual, especially around here."
"I think I'm starting to get arthritis!" added Blitzen.

"Nonsense," Santa shouted through the howling wind. "You're a magical being. You don't get arthritis."

"Well, I'm stiffening up," snapped Blitzen.

"Me too," shouted Dancer.

"You can't get the staff these days," laughed Santa. "This lot are always complaining."

Leaving the storm up above them, Santa told Indy to level off. Deliveries started again and Santa began covering the many other countries and islands that made up the vast Asian continent.

"This continent is vast," said Indy. "I'm glad Bernard knows where we're going. My teeth are chattering so much, I'm finding it hard to hear him."

Santa began more deliveries and the reindeer were glad of a short rest.

"How are you doing, Bert?" asked Indy.

"Bearing up, but Blitzen is right, the cold gets to your bones. We're so exposed."

Santa returned in no time and hurried them along to the next stop, then the next, and before long they'd covered half of this immense continent. Up and down they went to all the houses of children who believed in Santa Claus.

Santa told them stories of years gone by, when he'd nearly got caught by children trying to get a glimpse of him. He also told them some sad stories of children who had no presents allocated to their name, but he still left them one. Parents were too busy sometimes to tell Santa what their children would like, but he always left them something special.

"I think what you do every Christmas Santa is truly amazing," said Indy. "Young children throughout the world wait patiently for you to visit their homes with gifts. Precious things, fun things to bring them joy and love from those most close to them."

The sleigh fell silent at Indy's words.

"Your right of course Indy! It's why I keep delivering Christmas presents every year, to bring joy," replied Santa.

Soon enough the the deliveries in Asia were done and everyone was amazed at Santa's stamina.

"Where are we off to next, Bernard?" asked Bert.

"To Africa my man, I can't wait to see the Sahara Desert. Did you realise Africa is surrounded by the Mediterranean Sea, the Red Sea, the Indian Ocean, and the Atlantic Ocean." said Bernard.

"Wow, that's amazing!" said Indy.

"I never in my life imagined that I'd see the world as I am doing tonight. Although covered in darkness, I can still see much more than I ever thought I would," gushed Sidney.

"It's magical," whispered Toto.

"I'm so glad I came now," muttered Marmaduke. "I admit to being a bit scared about coming along at first, but I wouldn't have missed this for the world."
Approaching Africa, they could make out patches of lights in the cities and darkness in other areas.
"I love the different cultures around the world, the uniqueness of how Christmas is celebrated is fascinating," commented Blossom.

"In Africa, Christmas is all about festive concerts, sunny outdoor feasts and Christmas street parades," Santa told them

"Wow, really!" replied Blossom, "it sounds like so much fun!"

"Now, everyone, enough chatter, onto the first delivery," Santa told him.

Onward the troop went from town to city, then out into the isolated places. There were so many different buildings Santa delivered to, some large, some more humble, but all held children waiting for presents.

It had been an eye opener for Indy to see all the different parts of the world and the difference in children's homes. He really hoped each home would be filled with happiness and love.

"This is an amazing adventure, Indy my friend," shouted Bert, from behind him. "Thank you so much for letting me come along. You've made a old shapeshifter very happy."

Time moved on as Santa continued delivering presents throughout Africa and the outlying islands. The troop really enjoyed their journey through this large continent, but they needed to get to Europe to keep to Santa's delivery schedule.

Over the Mediterranean Sea, the sleigh flew, spotting the different ships and fishing trawlers out on the sea.

Chapter 7

"Santa?" asked Blossom. "Can I go with you on this delivery?"

"Me too!" said Sidney.

"Only you two and remember to be quiet and not cause any problems," replied Santa.

Jim passed the presents to Santa and winked at Blossom.

"Do be really careful. He'll go mad if you wake the house." added Jim.

"I will, I promise."

Creeping through the house, it all looked so beautiful and smelt of fresh fruit, cakes and breads. All the lights were off, other than a soft glow from a small outside light. On the table near the Christmas tree stood a glass of something and a piece of cake and a carrot.

"The cake and wine are for me and the carrot is for the reindeer. A lovely tradition. I sometimes drink the wine, otherwise I keep my bottle topped up," explained Santa, producing a rather large bottle from a deep pocket in his coat. "This lasts me all year when I get back home."

"It's all so magical," whispered Blossom.

"It is," replied Sidney with a swish of his tail.

His tail caught the empty glass and it fell towards the tiled floor.

"Oh no!" cried Santa.

But in a flash, Jim appeared and caught the glass and put it back on the table.

"My goodness Jim, where did you come from?" said Sidney.

"I thought I ought to check out your first Christmas delivery, just in case of disaster."

"I'm so glad you did," said Sidney.

Getting back on board the sleigh, Jim could tell Sidney was still flustered and he stroked his back and told him not to worry.

"On one of my deliveries with Santa, I made such a noise, Santa had to leave really quickly. I had to make a noise like a cat and shoot out the back door behind the Christmas Tree. Thankfully, no one came down straight away and we'd took off by the time the lights came on," explained Jim.

Onward Santa went, to so many countries, with houses filled with children dreaming of him delivering their presents. Each country having their own traditions.

They were flying high above the Alps with the snow topped mountains glistening like diamonds in the moonlight.

Sidney, Blossom, Marmaduke and Toto leant over the side of the sleigh to capture every glorious moment.

Leaving this beautiful scene behind, the reindeer made their descent to the next stop. Santa had the first presents in his hands and walked slowly to the first house. Suddenly the door opened and a young boy stood there smiling. He saw Santa and didn't seem at all surprised and ran past him to the sleigh.

"Hallo Jim, du hast heute Abend ein paar neue Helfer," said the little boy.

"What did he say?" asked Indy.

"He said, hello Jim, you've got some new helpers tonight."

"How did he know we were different helpers?" asked Indy.

"He has been visiting us every year for the past five years. The first time Santa visited this home many years ago, the boy's great-great-grandfather, four years old at the time, was found sleeping under the Christmas tree. He woke up and saw Santa leave the house and squealed with glee and looked out the long window as we left," explained Jim.

"Wow, how amazing!" gushed Toto.

Jim continued. "This home has been owned by the same family ever since and the youngest child of the family always comes to greet us, until a certain age."

The young boy still sitting next to Jim patted the heads of the animals in the back. Then he jumped down off the sleigh, shaking hands with Santa as he skipped to his door and closed it quietly.

Santa carried on delivering to each home in turn, up and down the sleigh flew until it reached Norway. Santa decided to give everyone a short rest and he produced some treats for the crew, which were gratefully received.

Indy had to admit to Bernard, the rook, he'd never been shapeshifted for this long before. Although he enjoyed being a reindeer, he hoped he would be able to change back when the adventure was over.

"I do like being leading reindeer!" said Indy, "but it's hard work, so please let Rudolph know that I admire him very much and hope one day to meet him in person."

"Hurrah," exclaimed Jim, "I will tell him on our return."

When the next upload of presents came, a note attached to a plain box said Rudolph is feeling much better and Comet was being looked after by the vets for a chest infection.

Bernard rested his head on Indy's antler's, letting out a sigh.

"I hope I can last out for the rest of the journey," said Bernard.

Santa came round to Bernard and unclipped his harness.

"You're not letting me go are you? I can finish the trip, I promise!" Bernard cried.

"I know you can my friend, but go for a fly around the fjords for a few minutes, get the wind under your wings and you'll feel much better," Santa told him.

So up he flew, above the fjord and surrounding mountains, finally landing back next to Santa, who lifted him into his harness ready for the rest of the trip.

"Feel better?" asked Indy.

"Oh yes, I feel amazing," Bernard replied.

"Santa said we will soon be going to the United Kingdom and Ireland. I can't wait to see our homeland again," said Bert.

"The Channel Islands first," added Bernard.

"Lead the way Indy, and enjoy the ride to our next delivery," prompted Santa.

Up they flew again, Indy out front with Bernard squawking directions to him, followed by Dasher, Dancer, Prancer, Vixen, Bert, Cupid, Donner and Blitzen.

"It's really good of you guys to help us out," said Donner. "It's tiring work but we are happy to do it."

"Our pleasure," replied Indy. "To work with such well known reindeers is an honour and a privilege."

"One day, we could ask Santa if you could visit us in the North Pole and you could meet Rudolph and the rest of the elves," beamed Cupid.

Catching Cupid's words on the wind, Toto clapped his paws together and shouted to Santa.

"Santa, I'd really love to come and visit you, and the elves' workshop."

"We all would!" the others cried.

"Let's get these presents delivered and then we can talk about it," replied Santa.

Chapter 8

Up and down they went, taking in all parts of the United Kingdom's of England, Wales, Scotland, Northern Ireland and Southern Ireland and all the islands around them.

"How are we doing for time, Jim?" asked Santa.

"We're making good time," he replied.

"North and South America, Canada, Hawaii and the Caribbean islands and we're nearly done," said Santa. "Then check the delivery manifest just in case."

"It's quite a long journey buddies," Indy said, first to Bernard, then to Bert and the other reindeers.

Santa turned to the cats and Toto and smiled at their sleepy faces.

"My sweet darlings, Sidney, Blossom, Marmaduke and Toto, I think you should take the journey time to catch up a bit on sleep," Santa told them.

"Thank you so much Santa," yawned Marmaduke. "I'm not as young as I used to be and I'm struggling to keep my eyes open."

All settled down across the back seat of the sleigh. Sidney and Blossom snuggled up together, and Marmaduke and Toto occupied the rest of the seat and were soon fast asleep.

Bernard announced that everyone needed to be ready to take flight, as he'd already picked his route across the Atlantic Ocean.

"We're ready and raring to go," said Donner, and the other reindeer all agreed.

Indy was in his element and said just that to Bernard.

"I see now why you love being a bird. The things you see from up here are amazing. No wonder you and your kind welcome each dawn with a song."

"I am so pleased you've been able to see and feel what it's like to fly," expressed Bernard.

Jim turned to look at his sleeping friends, smiling at their peaceful faces and listening to the different tones of Marmaduke's snoring.

Santa, in turn, smiled at Jim's obvious delight at having new friends.

"You are enjoying yourself, aren't you Jim?" said Santa. "I know you came here to disrupt my deliveries, but I think you've learnt a valuable lesson."

"I have," replied Jim. "I promise to never do anything like that again, and I know that the other elves will follow suit. I am sorry I doubted you when you said you couldn't pay more than you do."

Time passed quickly and Indy saw the outline of the Canadian coast taking in Nova Scotia, but Iceland then Greenland were their first two stops.

"I am blown away by all the islands that make up the earth's continents, some large and some small," gushed Indy.

"We need to start our descent to the first stop Indy," advised Bernard.

Indy led with the other reindeer, following him in a winding motion to decelerate.

"How majestic they look!" said Santa. "Indy and Bert fit right in."

"Don't say that to Rudolph or Comet, they'll worry about who you'll ask to fly next year." exclaimed Jim with a smile.

"Time to wake those four up in the back, we need them to sort the presents out," suggested Jim. "Is that the cutest scene ever, but it's time to wake them."

Bleary-eyed and yawning, Toto woke the others.

"Wow, look at those lights below, how amazing. Let's get the presents ready." Toto said.

First stop Iceland, then Greenland. Deliveries were swift and sure and soon they were onto Nova Scotia and then the Canadian mainland.

"We're making really good time crew, I'm so proud of you all," praised Santa.

Completing the Canadian mainland, the crew made their final stop in Canada at Niagara Falls, where it bordered with North America.

There was a sudden clanking noise and Santa looked worried.

"Not the sleigh undercarriage again. Why does it do this?" cried Jim.

"I think we overload it to be honest," replied Santa. "I'll have to re-adjust the upload weight when we get back."

"Bernard, look for a landing place," said Indy.

He picked what he thought was the perfect place for repairs.

Getting off the sleigh, Jim and Santa began looking for the problem.

"What the heck are you doing? You can't park there!" snapped a grumpy looking man in a uniform carrying a clipboard.

Santa got out from underneath the sleigh, banging his head as he did so.

"Where's your papers?" the uniformed man asked.

"What papers did you want. The presents are already wrapped," replied Santa.

"I am the border control officer and you will do what I ask," he demanded.

"Flipping heck, he's a bit grouchy. What's his problem?" whispered Toto to Sidney.

Irritated, Santa asked what papers he required?

"Your passport, of course, and have the animals been vaccinated against rabies. It must be over 30 days ago?" the officer shouted.

"How rude!" sniffed Prancer. "I'll have him know I'm in perfect condition."

Indy had to agree, what was this guy thinking?

"I haven't got time for this!" cried Santa. "I have Christmas presents to deliver and you are making us late!"

"What is your name and address, sir?" asked the officer.

"What's yours?" snapped Santa.

"I don't need to tell you!" he replied.

"You give me yours and I'll give you mine," said Santa cheekily.

"Oh for goodness sake! My name is Hank. D. Littlebottom."

Jim had to stifle a giggle as he whispered to Santa that the sleigh was now ready to go.

"Thank you Hank. My name is Santa Claus and I live in the North Pole."

"Oh, very funny!" snapped Hank. "Where's Rudolph then? This guy hasn't got a red nose for a start!"

"I'm hurt," said Indy. "I can't help it if my nose isn't red. I'm just standing in for this year."

"Who said that?" hissed Hank.

Realising that Hank could hear Indy, the entire crew shouted "Me."

Hank was startled by the sheer noise of their voices.

"Is there a problem, Hank?" asked another uniformed officer.

At first he couldn't speak, then he held his head in his hands and groaned.

"This guy says he's Santa Claus and those reindeer just spoke to me." said Hank.

"Hi Santa, it's Rowland, don't worry I'll look after Hank. It's been a while since I've seen you in person."

"Thanks Rowland, everybody get ready for takeoff. Indy take flight."

Chapter 9

The sleigh lifted off quietly and they were over the border into North America.

Indy fought his way through hail and snow near New York, but he had got used to it when he was in Greenland and over the Rocky Mountains.

The deliveries were on time, and Santa was on a roll. This merry band of Christmas travellers would be going throughout North America. They even had to make a stop at the White House in Washington DC, as the President of the United States was there with his extended family, including great grandchildren. They would make that their final stop in the capital.

Jim was a bit nervous about them coming into land at the White House. He knew the security would be tight, so he voiced his concerns.

"I'm not particularly happy about us landing at the White House," expressed Jim the elf. "Who knows what the security guys might throw at us."

"I can help with that," replied Indy.

"Really, how?" asked Jim.

"I have the magical ability to make things invisible," he said

"Wow!" exclaimed Donner.

"Wow indeed!" added Jim.

"We will still be visible to each other, but no one else," explained Indy.

"How will we know if we are invisible to others then?" asked Santa.

"I think we'd soon find out!" said Jim.

"That's a bit dangerous!" grumbled Vixen. "I don't want to get hurt. I have children back home to care for."

"I understand," said Indy. "Look I'll pass by one of those glass buildings over in the distance and see if we have a reflection. Is that ok?"

"Alright," answered Vixen.

Indy dug deep inside his soul and summoned the magic required to make them all invisible to the outside world. It covered them all and he was sure that they were invisible. Yet to be sure, he passed a row of buildings that were in darkness with just the street lights for reflection. The crew and Santa were amazed to see there was no reflection.

"Amazing!" cried out Cupid.

Off they sped to the White House having dropped off presents at all the other houses, who had young children inside. Slowly they circled the huge building, looking for a suitable place to land. Having found it, they landed without any trouble with security. Santa picked up the presents and walked past a few guards and was glad of Indy's extended invisibility magic.

One of the guards commented to his colleague saying, "I remember when I was small, waking up to find presents at the end of my bed from Santa. I sometimes wish I was that young again."

"Have you gone soft, Eddie, whatever made you say that?"

"I don't know, it was just a feeling I suddenly got," answered Eddie.

"Well concentrate Eddie, for goodness sake," said his colleague.

Santa had to smile at what Eddie had said, as his presence always made the children dream of Christmas morning.

Using the universal key Santa entered the living room, then disaster. A German shepherd jumped out in front of him with snarling teeth. Santa was frozen to the spot. The dog came nearer to him with its eyes blazing with anger.

"Flipping heck, nice doggy, nice doggy," Santa said, bending down to pacify it, but it jumped at him.
In a panic Santa just threw the presents onto the sofa and ran for it. The dog pursued him barking loudly. He ran faster, but the dog bit at his bottom and ripped off a portion of his trousers, which the dog shook out of its mouth. Santa ran passed the guards who tried to stop the dog chasing what appeared to be nothing at all.

Finally, Santa jumped on to the sleigh and Indy and the other reindeer took flight immediately. As they did, Eddie swore he could see Santa and his sleigh in the distance, but put it down to his anxiety of having to calm the presidents dog down. Yet what was this red velvet piece of material he found later.

Once everyone had calmed Santa down, they continued to the next state.

"I knew the United States was big Bernard, but to see it from up here reminds you that although the United Kingdom is small in comparison, it's got a big personality," gushed Indy.

"It's incredible how Santa remembers every island and outpost, however remote. Yet, he still stays on time when reaching the next stop," commented Marmaduke.

Santa went throughout Mexico and then it was onto South America. Taking in the outlying islands.

Indy asked Santa if they could see the Amazon and Machu Picchu and Santa agreed. All over South America they flew, so many homes to deliver to. Yet, it was soon time to fly back to England. Santa needed to drop off his extra crew and catch a lift with Hugo to the North Pole.

Santa decided that before they finally flew back to England, it was important to have some quality time to celebrate what had been achieved. It had meant so much to Santa, Jim, and the other reindeer that Indy and his friends had helped them in their hour of need. Selflessly, this collection of friends had taken on a journey with no experience or knowledge of what it may physically entail.

"You are our heroes," Prancer announced.

"You certainly are!" exclaimed Santa.

"Three cheers for our wonderful friends," added Blitzen.

"Hurray, Hurray, Hurray," they all shouted.

Indy spoke first. "I think I can speak for us all, when I say it has been both a pleasure and a privilege to have worked with you all. I for one, will always remember this time we have spent together. To be part of this Christmas tradition, which brings joy to so many children from across the world is an experience we will never forget."

"Well said," agreed Bert.

"Can we come again?" asked Toto, Marmaduke, Blossom and Sidney in unison.

"I'm in," cackled Bernard.

The crew huddled around Santa.

"I love you all so much and I know I can rely on you to help me again. I promise, one day very soon, I will come along and whisk you off to the North Pole to meet everyone" sobbed Santa.

"Time we were getting back Santa," suggested Jim.

"Ah yes, we mustn't be seen leaving here. Is everyone secured?"

Everyone replied with "yes Santa."

"Up and away, Indy," said Santa.

Bernard set his internal satnav towards home and they were soon flying across the sky towards the United Kingdom and home to the wood.

"I feel sad and happy at the same time," said Sidney. "Sad to be near the end of this amazing adventure, but happy to be going home."

"Me too," added Toto.

"Me three," said Marmaduke, "but what stories I have to tell!"

"Let's put our paws together," suggested Blossom.

"We were all friends before we began this adventure," said Blossom, "but I think we now share a bond that surpasses that. We have a special relationship with each other and with Indy, Bert and Bernard, a love and friendship special to us all."

"Your going to make me cry," sniffed Toto.

Time passed and finally Bernard said he could see the wood in the distance.

"Flipping heck Bernard! How can you see it from here!" exclaimed Indy.

"I have a birds eye view," cackled Bernard.

There was a united groan at Bernards attempt at a joke.

On Bernards instruction, they headed for a clearing near Mabel's house.

The sleigh floated calmly into the clearing and some animals had to run for cover. Yet, as soon as the sleigh came to a stop, they came forward. having been alerted by Mabel's remarkable awareness of their presence in the vicinity.

There to meet them were Mabel, Sedgwick, Bernard's cousin, Toto's family, Katie and Martin Indy's human parents, and Hugo and Harry waiting to take Santa and his crew back to the North Pole.

Everyone huddled round Santa and his crew and many were fascinated by the elf and the reindeer. Many thank you's and goodbyes were exchanged and tears flowed, but it was soon time for Santa to leave. Bernard and Sedgwick escorting them back to Hugo's shuttle craft.

Indy shapeshifted back to a hamster and crawled up into Katie hands. Toto joined his family and Bert, now a man again joined Marmaduke, Sidney and Blossom, and went back towards Katie and Martin's house.

Indy, Katie and Martin said their farewells and Bert and his friends set off home. Indy lay warming himself by the fire and was soon asleep dreaming of how wonderful his adventure had been.

The End.

About the author

Lesley Nelson was born in 1957 in Nottingham, England. As a child she spent many hours at the city's historical Wollaton Hall and its enchanting grounds, a place which lends itself to the imaginings of a young girl who loved stories.

Added to this was her love of animals. She adored watching Johnny Morris in the 1960's children's zoology series. Johnny would interact with the animals at Bristol Zoo with voice-overs that perfectly suited each animal. These memories are inspiring stories years later.

A chance meeting with Indy, a pet hamster who belongs to her friend Katie inspired her first story The Adventures of Indy, the shape shifting hamster. Now we have a special edition called How Indy and his friends save Christmas. Another opportunity for Indy and his friends to have an exciting adventure.

Printed in Great Britain
by Amazon

32129598R00036